D0646462

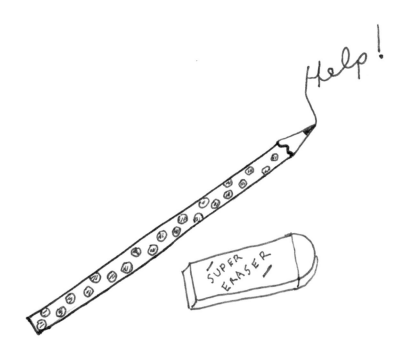

I WISH
I COULD

GROUNDWOOD BOOKS   HOUSE OF ANANSI PRESS   TORONTO   BERKELEY

WITHDRAWN

DRAW

WORDS AND

(BAD) PICTURES BY

Cary Fagan

Once more for my mother,
who liked to draw with me.

Copyright © 2014 by Cary Fagan
Published in Canada and the USA in 2014 by Groundwood Books

All rights reserved. No part of this publication may be reproduced, stored in
a retrieval system or transmitted, in any form or by any means, without the
prior written consent of the publisher or a license from The Canadian
Copyright Licensing Agency (Access Copyright). For an Access Copyright
license, visit www.accesscopyright.ca or call toll free to 1-800-893-5777.

Groundwood Books / House of Anansi Press
110 Spadina Avenue, Suite 801, Toronto, Ontario M5V 2K4
or c/o Publishers Group West
1700 Fourth Street, Berkeley, CA 94710

We acknowledge for their financial support of our publishing program the
Canada Council for the Arts, the Government of Canada through the Canada
Book Fund (CBF) and the Ontario Arts Council.

 Canada Council   Conseil des Arts    ONTARIO ARTS COUNCIL
for the Arts   du Canada   CONSEIL DES ARTS DE L'ONTARIO

Library and Archives Canada Cataloguing in Publication
Fagan, Cary, author   I wish I could draw / Cary Fagan.
Issued in print and electronic formats. ISBN 978-1-55498-318-6 (bound).—
ISBN 978-1-55498-319-3 (html)
I. Title.
PS8561.A375I2 2014   jC813'.54   C2013-905588-6
C2013-905589-4

The illustrations were done in Sharpie pen on
Daler-Rowney HeavyWeight paper.
Design by Michael Solomon
Printed and bound in China

I really, really wish I could draw.

But I don't think I can. I think I stink at drawing.

Let me show you.

Here is a drawing of me.

It doesn't look like me. Okay, I do have curly hair and I wear glasses. But the rest is no good at all. Look! I even put my hands behind my back because it's so hard for me to draw hands.

Let me show you again.

I will try to draw a "Still Life."

Do you know what a "Still Life" is? It's a drawing of a bunch of flowers, or some fruit in a bowl, or maybe a bowl or a teapot and a plate of cheese. Artists draw them all the time. Don't ask me why.

So here are the things I need.

1. Bowl

2. Teapot

3. Fruit

4. Drapery

And here is my drawing.

Ha! You call that a "Still Life"? Maybe it
isn't terrible, but it is not very good. It isn't like
a drawing by a *real* artist.

I'm so mad I can't draw that I look like this.

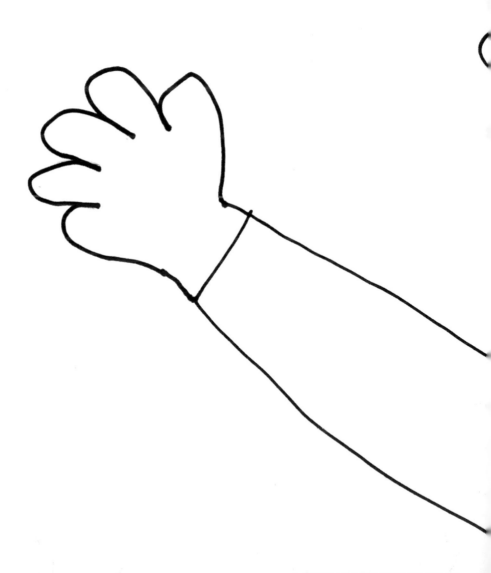

On the other hand, a bowl of fruit is pretty boring. I wonder what will happen if I try to draw things that I actually *like*.

Okay, let's find out.

A bird sitting on a nest.

An exploding star.

A movie star riding a bicycle.

A double-scoop chocolate ice cream cone.

Hmm, they're not too bad. It *does* help to draw something I like.

Maybe my pictures will look even better if I use them to tell a story. After all, I like making up stories.

I just need a place to begin. How about a house? A house isn't so hard to draw. It's just a triangle on top of a square.

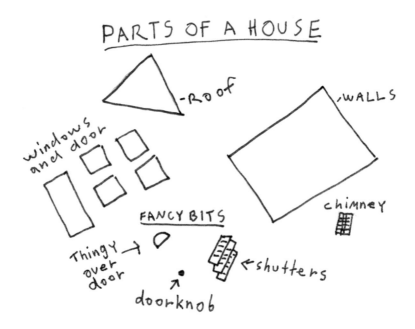

PARTS OF A HOUSE

-Roof

,WALLS

windows and door

FANCY BITS

chimney

Thingy → over door

← shutters

doorknob

So...

Once upon a time, a boy named Cary (that's me) was sitting in his house eating a double-scoop chocolate ice cream cone.

So far, so good. Now I need something exciting to happen.

Suddenly a dragon appeared wanting to eat the ice cream cone!

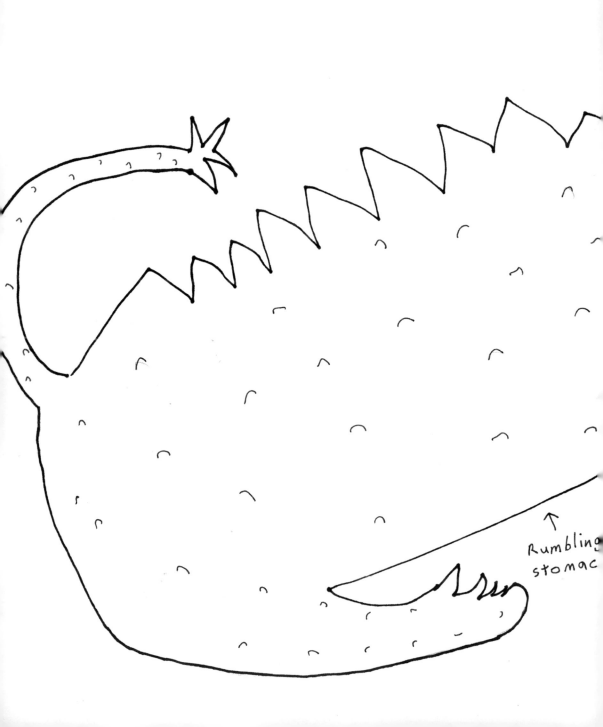

Rumbling
stomac

Yikes! What a predicament.
Now how do I rescue my family?
Hit the dragon with a shoe?
Paint its tail pink?
Throw a can of dragon chow
down the street?
I've got it!

Cary knew that dragons didn't like noise.
So he came out of the house and played his
mandolin really loud!

Tiny but highly sensitive earhole

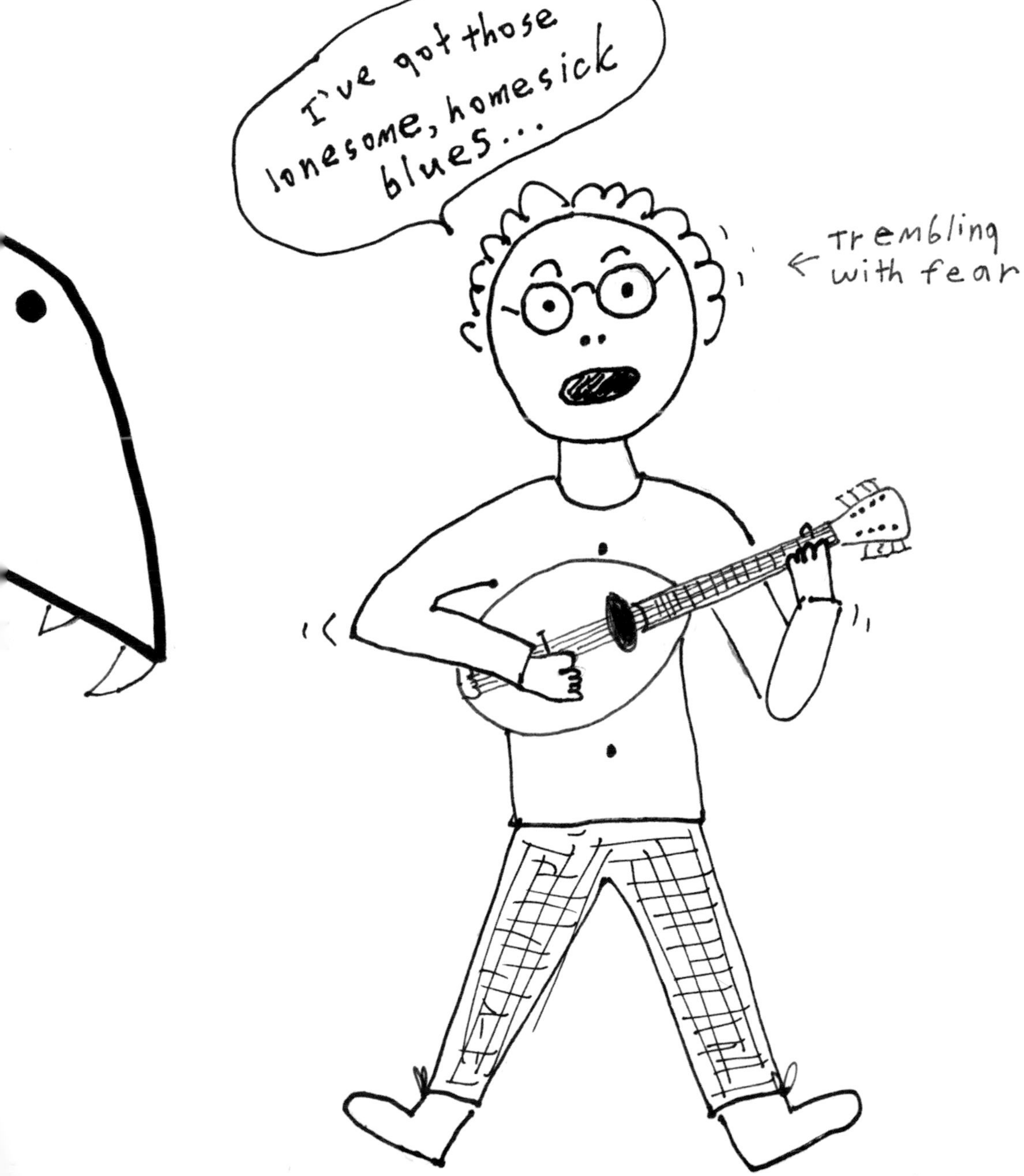
I've got those lonesome, homesick blues...
trembling with fear

HOT!

EARTH

satellite

OCEAN

The dragon ran away!

The town was so thankful that the mayor
gave Cary a big medal.
"Aw, shucks," Cary said. "It was nothing."
The crowd cheered.

Actual
size! →

LOCAL HERO
SMART ◆ BRAVE

FREE RIDE ON ANY BUS!

Bravo!

From then on, nobody complained when Cary sat on the porch and played his mandolin.
The end.

A story with pictures is fun to make. I could even make a book out of it. That would be pretty cool.

ITTLE ◆ BOOKSHOP

WINNER!
Dill Pickle
Award

Soon to be
a major motion
picture
(or a puppet show)

BAD
DRAGON!

BY CARY FAGAN

So if I really like to draw, does that make me an artist? What if some day my self-portrait hangs in a big museum?

Well, it's fun to imagine.
Mostly though, it's fun to draw
all these stinky pictures!

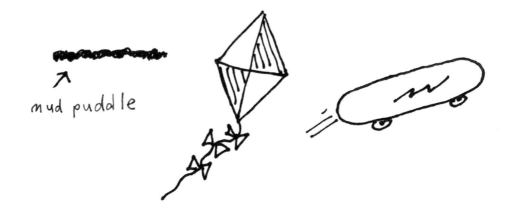

Easy landscape #1: mountains

So thanks for looking.
Now you can go and draw
your own stinky pictures.
And maybe some day you'll
show them to me!

These are cool!

you!

Dog (or lizard or pig...)

Easy landscape #2:
trees

31901055559126